WORM WEATHER

For Mom, who brought us on walks in all kinds of weather—JT

For Hayley and Henry—MH

GROSSET & DUNLAP
Penguin Young Readers Group
An Imprint of Penguin Random House LLC

Text copyright © 2015 by Jean Taft. Illustrations copyright © 2015 by Penguin Random House LLC. All rights reserved. Published by Grosset & Dunlap, an imprint of Penguin Random House LLC, 345 Hudson Street, New York, New York 10014. GROSSET & DUNLAP is a trademark of Penguin Random House LLC. Manufactured in China.

Library of Congress Control Number: 2014044243

ISBN 978-0-448-48740-3 (pbk)   19
ISBN 978-0-448-48741-0 (hc)   10 9 8 7 6 5 4 3 2 1

WORM WEATHER

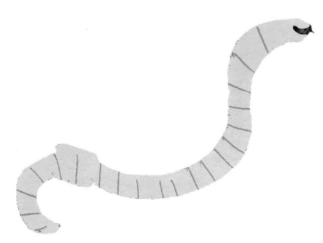

by Jean Taft
illustrated by Matt Hunt

Grosset & Dunlap
An Imprint of Penguin Random House

Drip, drop,
skip and hop.

Splish, splash,
sidewalk dash!

Worm, worm,
wiggle, squirm.

Worm weather!

Coat.

Hat.

Rain goes **splat!**

Boots jump,

old tree stump.

Big STOMP,

puddle swamp.

Almost!

Dark cloud.

Bright flash,

THUNDER,
CRASH!

Quick, race!
Pizza place!

Drip-dry.

Pizza pie.

Sun pops,

drizzle stops.

Birds fly,

rainbow sky!

Run, sing,

playground! Swing!

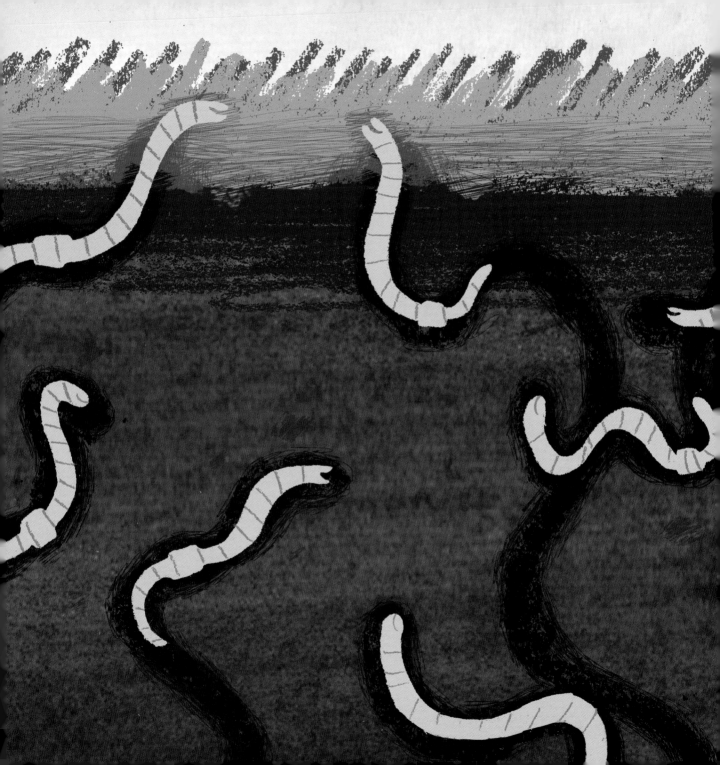

Worm, worm,
wiggle, squirm.

It's worm weather!